Billy Bonkers

NOT MY PANTS!

For xxx

G.A.

With special thanks to Rachel Moss

ORCHARD BOOKS
338 Euston Road, London NW1 3BH
Orchard Books Australia
Level 17/207 Kent Street, Sydney, NSW 2000

First published in 2012 by Orchard Books

ISBN 978 1 40831 465 4

Text © Giles Andreae 2012
Cover illustration © Nick Sharratt 2012
Inside illustrations © Orchard Books 2012

The right of Giles Andreae to be identified as the author
of this work has been asserted by him in accordance
with the Copyright, Designs and Patents Act, 1988.

A CIP catalogue record for this book is available from the British Library.

1 3 5 7 9 10 8 6 4 2

Printed in Great Britain

Orchard Books is a division of Hachette Children's Books,
an Hachette UK company.

www.hachette.co.uk

Billy Bonkers

NOT MY PANTS!

Giles Andreae

ORCHARD

Giles Andreae is an award-winning
children's author who has written many
bestselling picture books, including
Giraffes Can't Dance and *Commotion in the Ocean*.

He is probably most famous as the creator of
the phenomenally successful Purple Ronnie,
Britain's favourite stickman. Giles lives by the river
near Oxford with his wife and four young children.

Contents

Billy Bonkers

and the
Rage Cage

William Benedict Bertwhistle Bonkers was not happy.

Now, don't get me wrong. William – or Billy, as most people called him – wasn't a moody boy. Usually he was very easy to please – especially if there were a few cakes and sweets and pork pies within arms' length.

But today Billy was most definitely *not* OK.

At first, everything was fine. He got up. He fed his goldfish, Snapper. Then he opened his top drawer and noticed that his pants were looking a bit old. He twanged the elastic experimentally on a couple of pairs. It was getting very loose.

"Mum!" Billy called out. "I think I need some new pants!"

And that's when things started to go wrong.

You see, Mrs Bonkers had been reading a book called *Melvin Marvel's Guide to Saving Money*.

Melvin Marvel was a hunky, tanned TV presenter, and Mrs Bonkers enjoyed watching his show very much.

"Melvin Marvel says that older children's clothes should be passed to their younger siblings when they get too small, instead of buying new ones," Mum said, bustling into Billy's bedroom. "I think we should try it."

Billy gulped. She couldn't mean what he thought she meant. Could she?

"Er, Mum," he said. "Haven't you forgotten something? I don't *have* any older brothers. I've got one annoying older sister."

"That doesn't matter," Mrs Bonkers said.

"Betty has some pants that she's only worn a few times, and she's too big for them now."

She popped next door into Betty's room and then came back holding something pink and frilly. Billy stared at the pants. They were covered in pictures of kittens, which seemed to be staring right back at him. He put his hand on Mrs Bonkers's shoulder and patted it gently.

"Mum," he said. "I think you've gone a bit nuts. Shall I call the doctor?"

"Nonsense," said Mrs Bonkers, putting the ghastly pants on Billy's chair. "I won't hear another word about it. Melvin Marvel knows best. You can use these until you can't wear them any more. Just put them on and come downstairs."

Billy gaped at her. She couldn't be serious …could she?

Mrs Bonkers began pulling out all Billy's baggy old pants from his drawer.

"Let's just think about this for a minute," said Billy, snatching a couple of his now *very precious* pairs away from her.

"All right," said Mum. "You can keep those. That's three pairs: one for today, one for tomorrow and Betty's pair for school on Monday. Then I'll do a wash. Now get dressed and come to the kitchen for Dad's birthday breakfast."

As Mrs Bonkers trotted downstairs, Billy gritted his teeth and thought about what he'd like to say to Melvin Marvel if he ever met him. I'm afraid that it wasn't very polite.

The Rage Cage

He pulled on the pants with the fewest holes and the tightest elastic, and wished that he'd never said anything. There was *no way* that he was going to wear Betty's pants. But Mrs Bonkers had said that he would have to wear them until he couldn't wear them any more. How was he going to get around that?

The plan of how to avoid wearing Betty's pants popped into Billy's head like a light bulb getting very slightly brighter. Somehow, Billy had to make sure that the pants met with an *unfortunate accident*. And that meant waiting for the *perfect opportunity*. He had two days to get rid of them, else he'd be wearing them to school on Monday morning.

PING!

And that was about the worst thing Billy could imagine *ever* happening to him.

He shoved the disgusting pants into his pocket and then realised that his belly was making annoyed gurgling noises.

Right. Breakfast! thought Billy.

***

"Happy birthday, Dad," said Billy, bouncing into his seat at the kitchen table.

"Look at this!" said Mr Bonkers, waving a card in the air. It said *Happy 50th Birthday* on the front in big gold letters. "How could Great Aunt Ermintrude think I'm fifty?

I don't look fifty! I don't know what great aunts are coming to. She's gone mad. I'm nowhere near fifty."

"No," said Billy with a grin. "Not until next year, anyway."

Mr Bonkers put the card face down on the table and picked up the newspaper. There was a picture of a lady in a bikini inside that he thought might take his mind off things.

"Right," said Mrs Bonkers. "What would you like for your special birthday breakfast, Sausage?"

"Sausage" wasn't a breakfast suggestion. It was what Mrs Bonkers called her husband.

She only called him by his real name when she was feeling especially exasperated. (Billy understood this because his father's real name was dreadful. He wasn't called Dreadful, you understand. He was called Nigel. Which is worse.)

"Mmm," said Mr Bonkers, licking his lips thoughtfully. "What do you think about sausages and bacon?"

"And eggs and kippers and fried mushrooms and eggy bread and grilled tomatoes and beans?" added Billy without pausing for breath. "Birthday breakfasts are the best!"

"Coming up," said Mrs Bonkers.

"Lovely, Piglet," said Mr Bonkers, rustling his newspaper.

Mr Bonkers called his wife Piglet. Billy had never found out why. After all, her real name was Marjorie. Piglet was *way* more embarrassing.

The Rage Cage

While he was waiting for the birthday breakfast, Billy poured himself a bowl of dry porridge oats to keep him going. You or I would add milk, but not Billy. He was what his mother liked to call "inventive", and what his sister liked to call "a *weirdo*".

"Hello, *weirdo*. Morning, Dad," said Betty as she came downstairs and sat at the kitchen table. "Happy birthday. Have you decided what we're going to do today?"

It was a Bonkers family tradition that on your birthday you could decide what everyone did for the day. Sometimes, Mrs Bonkers wished that it wasn't a Bonkers family tradition. She could have done without the year that Billy decided to go to a water park. Mr Bonkers had whizzed down a child-sized water chute, flown out of it halfway down and ended up on the roof of a hot-dog stand. And she wouldn't have minded missing out on the year that Betty chose to go ice-skating. Mr Bonkers had attempted a pirouette in the middle of the rink and fifteen people had ended up in hospital. But a tradition is a tradition, and there was no getting away from it.

"I haven't decided yet," Mr Bonkers replied. He cleared his throat a few times and turned the page of his newspaper. Then he sat up very straight in his seat. "Well!" he exclaimed. "Well well WELL!"

"Wharrirrit?" asked Billy, his cheeks full of porridge.

If you're thinking that it's rude to talk with your mouth full, you're quite right, but I'm afraid Billy did it often. He knew that if he only spoke when he wasn't eating, he'd hardly say anything at all.

"It's a very exciting advert," said Mr Bonkers, his eyes twinkling. "Just look at this, everyone!"

CALLING ALL SPEED DEMONS!
THE GRAND GO-KARTING CENTRE IS NOW OPEN.

Come and test your driving skills on our FANTASTIC new track!

"Do you think that's really such a good idea, Sausage?" asked Mrs Bonkers, taking her eyes off the scrambling eggs.

"Remember how you drove into that fence post last week?"

"Rubbish!" said Mr Bonkers. "It sprang up out of nowhere!"

"And you backed the car into a pond the week before that," Mrs Bonkers went on.

"Not my fault!" exclaimed Mr Bonkers.

"What sort of person puts a pond by the side of a road anyway? I don't know what the world is coming to!"

"I think it sounds brilliant!" said Billy, who was taking a breath between mouthfuls of dry porridge. It could be the perfect opportunity to get rid of the pants. They were already worse than his worst nightmare come true.

"Besides, it's my birthday," said Mr Bonkers, looking stubborn. "My birthday, my choice."

And Mrs Bonkers couldn't argue with that.

***

The Grand Go-Karting Centre was a few miles out of town. If you have ever been go-karting, you'll know that it's rather a smelly, noisy thing to do. That's why no one wants a go-karting track right next to their house. It's also why dads and kids love go-karting so much.

When the Bonkers family arrived at the go-karting centre, they were stopped by a spotty young lad who was wearing a red peaked cap and red overalls. Mr Bonkers wound down his window.

"We've come to test our driving skills

on your *FANTASTIC* new track," he said, remembering the advert.

"Not today, mate," said the lad. "We're holding the National Go-Karting Championships on the main track."

"Oh blast," said Mr Bonkers. "**Blast blast BLAST!**"

"*What* a shame," said Mrs Bonkers, who didn't look very sorry at all. "We'll just have to do something else for your birthday, Sausage."

"Oh, is it your birthday?" said the spotty boy. "Well, we do have a smaller, older track that isn't being used. I guess you could take the go-karts on that, seeing as it's a special day."

Mrs Bonkers frowned, but Billy and Betty bounced up and down on their seats. Mr Bonkers gave the lad a beaming smile.

"That's very kind," he said. "Lead on!"

They drove along a narrow lane towards the smaller track.

"Hey, what are you doing with my old pants?" Betty asked Billy.

A pink frill was poking out of his pocket.

"I wish everyone would stop talking

about *pants*," he whispered, feeling very uncomfortable. He pushed the pants back into his pocket, hoping his mother hadn't heard anything.

Just then Mr Bonkers stopped the car, and Betty was distracted by having to choose a go-kart. Soon, the Bonkers family were sitting inside four go-karts. The spotty lad, whose name was Percy, explained how to work them. Billy, Betty and Mrs Bonkers

listened very carefully, but Mr Bonkers was busy putting on his racing helmet, scarf and shades, and imagining that he was the winner of the National Championships that he could hear in the distance.

"I have to go back to the main entrance now," said Percy. "Have fun!"

He walked away and Mrs Bonkers looked anxiously at her husband.

"Did you listen to what he said?" she asked him.

"Yes, yes," said Mr Bonkers, waving his hand airily. "Well, I may have missed some of the finer points, but how hard can it be? Let's go!"

His engine roared and then he pulled away, leaving them in a cloud of dust.

"Wait for me!" yelled Billy, following as fast as he could.

"And me!" squealed Betty.

Mrs Bonkers rolled her eyes.

At first, everything went splendidly. The track was quite small, and the Bonkers family were the only ones using it. What could possibly go wrong?

"Woohoo!" shouted Mr Bonkers as his tyres squealed on the tarmac.

"Brilliant!" yelled Billy as he overtook Betty.

"Cool!" exclaimed Betty as she completed her tenth lap.

Even Mrs Bonkers was enjoying herself, and thinking that perhaps go-karting had been a good idea after all.

And that's when Mr Bonkers started to go faster.

I am sure that you know by now that most dads like winning. And some dads like winning *a lot*. Some men really *love* winning. Mr Bonkers was that sort of dad. He was what the organisers of the school Sports Day fathers' race called "a total menace".

Mr Bonkers liked playing tennis with Mrs Bonkers, because she could never remember the rules and he always won. He enjoyed beating Billy at Scrabble. (He never played Scrabble with Betty, because she knew more words than he did.) He even competed to find the fastest queue when he was shopping, and got very bad-tempered if another queue started moving more quickly. Billy never went shopping with him if he could help it.

Anyway, Mr Bonkers had decided to win, even if it wasn't a real race. Betty was close behind him, and he couldn't bear to be beaten by his own daughter. His foot pressed a little harder on the accelerator. And then a bit more. And then just a *smidge* more.

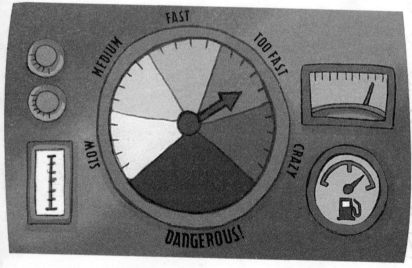

Meanwhile, Billy was listening to the commentary from the main track's loudspeaker system. It sounded as if a very exciting race had just started.

The Rage Cage

"THEY'RE OFF! And straightaway world-champion Scoot Petrolhead's souped-up Rage Cage has left the best of the rest standing. HE'S ON FIRE! Just look at Scoot go! But Zack Hack is coming up on the inside in his Killer Kart, and maybe Scoot should be worried. Zack's Killer Kart has just been through a major upgrade, and he's really picking up speed. Fans will know that Scoot Petrolhead's famous Rage Cage has never lost a race, but there's always a first time, right, Zack?"

At first, Billy was so interested in the commentary that he didn't notice how fast his dad's go-kart was going. Then he saw the smoke coming from Mr Bonkers's tyres.

"Dad, slow down!" Billy yelled.

Mr Bonkers gave a high-pitched squeak as his go-kart skidded sideways.

"Piiigggllettt!" he wailed as he hurtled into a hedge at the side of the track. His bumper fell off and bounced away.

"Lordy lorks!" squealed Mrs Bonkers, pulling up beside him. "Sausage!"

Betty stopped too, and together she and her mum pulled Mr Bonkers out of the hedge.

"Wonderful!" exclaimed Mr Bonkers, pulling a few leaves out of his ears. "Exhilarating! That was just what I was intending to do, of course!"

Billy could see that his dad was all right. And suddenly he remembered that he still had Betty's dreadful pants in his pocket.

This is my chance! thought Billy.

No one was looking. He could throw the pants into the hedge and no one would be any the wiser. Holding on to the wheel with his left hand, Billy thrust his right hand into his pocket and pulled out the pink frilly pants. But just at that moment...

His front wheel hit his dad's broken bumper, which had bounced onto the track.

The Rage Cage

Billy dropped the pants to grab the steering wheel, but the wind blew them right over his face.

"Help!" he cried.

All he could see were blurry pink kittens and white frills!

"Arghhh!" yelled Billy as he tried to control the go-kart and pull the pants off his face.

Swerving across the track like a lunatic, he juddered onto the grassy verge and smashed straight through a gate.

CRASH!

"**HUh-duh-duh-duh-duh-duh!**" said Billy as he was bounced around in his seat.

Scrabbling at the pants on his face, he tried to hit the brakes, but pumped the accelerator by mistake.

"**some-buh-buh-buh-body...HELP!**" he wailed as he thundered down a long, winding track. He felt as if his teeth were rattling around in his mouth.

At last he dragged the pants off his face – just as the go-kart crashed through a second gate and hit a boulder. Billy was catapulted into the air, still clutching the pink pants.

"HEEELLLPPP!"

Billy wailed as he flew across the big track.

Below, he could see a shiny black go-kart with "Rage Cage" written on the front and "Scoot Petrolhead" written on the back. It was the world champion's vehicle, and it was getting closer...and closer...and closer...until...

THWACK!

Billy landed inside the famous Rage Cage!

"Sorrysorrysorry!" Billy garbled, turning to look at Scoot Petrolhead.

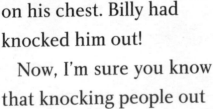

But the champion's hands had fallen from the wheel, and his head was drooping forwards on his chest. Billy had knocked him out!

Now, I'm sure you know that knocking people out is not a good thing to do. It can get you into a lot of trouble and it has all sorts of terrible consequences. However, on this occasion there wasn't a lot Billy could do about it. Scoot Petrolhead was out for the count, and someone had to drive the Rage Cage!

Pushing Scoot into the passenger seat, Billy settled into the driver's seat and grabbed the steering wheel, pressing his foot hard on the accelerator.

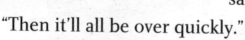

"I'll just drive it towards the finish line as fast I can," he said to himself. "Then it'll all be over quickly."

In the distance, he could hear the commentator babbling over the loudspeaker system.

The Rage Cage

"And I've never seen anything like it, ladies and gentlemen! Despite being hit by a freak boy-shaped meteor, Scoot Petrolhead is still in the lead! No sirree, a little thing like a meteor isn't going to stop this world-class driver! He's racing towards the finish line...but now Zack Hack is hot on his tail!"

Billy looked to his right and saw a lime-green go-kart creeping forwards. A thin, mean-looking driver was hunched over the wheel. Gritting his teeth, Billy pressed the accelerator to the floor.

"Folks, this is a race that'll go down in the history books!" the commentator was screaming. "It's Zack! No, it's Scoot! No, it's...it's...YES! Scoot Petrolhead retains his title! Go wild, people!"

Billy brought the go-kart to a stop as the sound of cheers and screams filled his ears. At that moment, Scoot Petrolhead groaned and raised his head.

"Wh-what happened?" he asked groggily.

"You won," said Billy, panting slightly.

Scoot shook his head and stared at the pink kitten knickers, which were still clutched in Billy's hand.

"Nice pants," Scoot said.

A hot tidal wave of embarrassment rolled over Billy. Hopefully you have never been unlucky enough to feel embarrassment like this. But having a racing driver think you wear pink kitten pants is roughly on the same scale as finding yourself in the middle of a maths lesson with no clothes on.

"THEY'RE NOT...MY...PANTS!"

Billy yelled.

He shoved them back into his pocket and clambered out of the go-kart. He'd have to think of another way to get rid of them – and fast.

Just then, Billy's family sprinted up to the Rage Cage. They had followed him down the winding track and seen exactly what had happened. Since then, Mr Bonkers and Betty had been cheering him on from the sidelines. (Mrs Bonkers had been hiding behind her scarf.)

"Billy, you were amazing!" exclaimed Betty, grinning at him. "Maybe those are lucky pants."

"I *really* don't think so!" said Billy.

"SPECTACULAR DRIVING!" bellowed Mr Bonkers at the top of his voice. "THAT'S MY BOY! TAUGHT HIM EVERYTHING HE KNOWS!"

"Oh my goodness!" wailed Mrs Bonkers, giving Billy a big hug. "You could have been killed! It's a miracle!"

"Is this your son?" asked Scoot Petrolhead, pulling himself out of the Rage Cage. "I'd like to shake you by the hand! You're a hero! If it hadn't been for you, I'd have lost the race!"

I'm sure you'll agree that it was very nice of Scoot Petrolhead to take this attitude. Of course, he *could* have said that if it hadn't been for Billy, he wouldn't have been knocked out in the first place.

"I hope you'll let me show you my gratitude properly," Scoot went on.

"Ooh!" said Mrs Bonkers. Visions of luxury restaurants and appearances in celebrity magazines danced in front of her mind's eye.

"I have my own private go-karting track at home," said Scoot, "and I would be delighted if you would come and ride on it with me – right now!"

Mrs Bonkers turned slightly green.

"I think I've had enough of go-karting for one day," she said.

But her family were already jumping up and down in excitement – even Mr Bonkers.

"Yes, PLEASE!" said Billy.

"Fantastic!" said Betty.

"Now that's what I call a treat!" said Mr Bonkers. "What a MAGNIFICENT birthday!"

THE END

Billy Bonkers

and the
Fart Fumigation

"Home sweet home," said Mr Bonkers as he parked outside his house and turned off the car engine.

"What a *wicked* day," sighed Billy happily.

It was Mr Bonkers's birthday, and the family had been to the local go-karting track. It had been a typical Bonkers day out.

Mr Bonkers had driven into a hedge, Billy had accidentally become a hero and then they had all been invited to a go-karting champion's personal racing track. Billy hadn't yet managed to get rid of his sister's awful pants, but he still had time to think of a new plan before school on Monday.

As they got out of the car, Mr Bonkers sniffed the air.

"I can smell burning," he said.

"Lordy lorks! The house is on fire!" gasped Mrs Bonkers.

"Mum, chill out," said Betty, also sniffing the air. "I think someone's having a barbecue."

The Fart Fumigation

"That's funny," said Billy. "It looks as if it's coming from our back garden."

"It *is* coming from our back garden!" Betty exclaimed. "Come on!"

They raced around to the back of the house – and then stopped in astonishment. Every single one of their neighbours was squashed into the Bonkers's garden!

Their barbecue was smoking, and Mrs Rocket from next door was handing around glasses of orange squash. Mrs Furball's mangy mongrel Cedric was slinking around, looking for unguarded food. Even some of the wasps from the infestation next door were buzzing over the fence. Mr Bonkers clutched his balding head.

"My barbecue!" he spluttered. "My garden! The neighbours have gone mad!"

That's when all the neighbours started singing *Happy Birthday*.

Have you ever heard your neighbours trying to sing the same song, at the same time, in the same tune? Unless you live next door to professional singers (which the Bonkers family didn't), it's like listening to fifty cats sharpening their claws on a metal post and meowing about it.

Billy and Betty stuck their fingers in their ears. But Mr Bonkers didn't seem to mind at all. A big smile spread over his face, and when Mrs Rocket gave him a birthday peck on the cheek, he blushed bright red.

"What a lovely dress, Candy," said Mrs Bonkers. "Isn't it a little chilly for the time of year?"

"Oh, I'm never cold!" said Candy Rocket with a tinkling laugh.

Roger Rocket, her husband, came bounding up to them carrying a huge present wrapped in red paper with a big gold bow.

"Happy birthday, Nigel!" he exclaimed. "This is from all the neighbours."

He handed the present to Mr Bonkers. Billy watched as Mr Bonkers ripped the paper off and gave a cry of delight.

"A leaf blower!" he shouted, gazing at the gadget. "Just what I've always wanted!"

He pulled it out of the box and the instructions fluttered to the floor.

"Don't you want to read those, Sausage?" asked Mrs Bonkers.

"No need, no need," said Mr Bonkers airily, switching it on.

"Er, Dad, when you blew up the vacuum cleaner you said that you'd look at the instructions next time you got a new gadget," Betty reminded him.

"Pish!" said Mr Bonkers. "Faulty wiring."

The leaf blower let out a jet of air that made him stagger backwards.

"Look!" he said, pointing to a large red button on the side of the machine. "It sucks as well as blows!"

Billy noticed that the leaf blower was pointing straight at Mrs Furball. Her wig was looking even more crooked than usual. Billy had a terrible thought. "Er, Dad," he whispered. "Maybe you should try that out later?"

"Nonsense!" said Mr Bonkers. "Balderdash and bunk! Perfect opportunity!"

He pressed the button and there was a loud clunk and a whirr. Then, with a groaning hum, the machine started to suck.

"Cranking it up to maximum!" declared

The Fart Fumigation

Mr Bonkers, who was having the time of his life.

"Look out, Mrs Furball!" cried Billy.

I don't really know how to describe the sound of an old lady's wig being sucked into a brand-new leaf blower. But it was something like…

SHWEEEOOOP!

Mrs Furball clutched her head in horror.

"Nigel!" cried Mrs Bonkers.

Mr Bonkers looked worried. His wife only called him by his real name when she was feeling especially annoyed. He turned the leaf blower off.

"Sorry, Mrs Furball," he said, pulling her wig out of the machine and brushing a few leaves off it. "No harm done."

Mrs Furball squashed it back onto her head and looked around for Cedric.

"What a machine!" said Mr Bonkers, gazing at the leaf blower with pride. "What a FANTASTIC birthday present!"

Just then there was a burst of laughter from over near the barbecue. All the dads had gathered around it, and Mr Rocket was holding up a spatula.

The Fart Fumigation

"Time to cook the sausages!" he said.

Mr Bonkers's barbecue was extremely old and rickety, and Mr Bonkers thought that he was the only one who could manage it. It had probably been around since cavemen discovered fire, and it was shakily held together with bits of tape and string.

Billy guessed that his father was desperate to barge past all the other dads and take over. (All dads think that they know how to cook the perfect barbecue sausage.) But to his surprise, a big smile spread across Mr Bonkers's face.

"Dad, are you OK?" Billy asked.

"OK?" Dad repeated, rubbing his hands together. "I'm better than OK, Billy my boy! I am about to teach you the ancient secret family recipe for Bonkers Barbecue Sausage Sauce!"

"That sounds brilliant, Dad," said Billy. "Er, what secret recipe?"

"Come on!" said Mr Bonkers. "This sauce will make me the king of the barbecue sausage forever! Roger Rocket will never be able to hold up a spatula again!"

Billy followed his dad into the kitchen, suddenly feeling a little bit nervous. He loved it when Mr Bonkers started experimenting, but whenever he tried to beat Mr Rocket at anything – well, things never quite seemed to go to plan.

"Right!" said Mr Bonkers, rubbing his hands together again. "Now let me think…"

He pulled the washing-up bowl out of the sink and opened all the kitchen cupboards. Billy watched as Tabasco, vinegar, brown sauce, chocolate topping and olive oil were emptied into the washing-up bowl.

"Um…Dad…are you sure those are the right amounts?" he asked.

When you're cooking, it is usually quite important to follow the instructions. Billy had seen his mum exploding steak-and-kidney pies often enough to know when something was going wrong.

But Mr Bonkers wasn't really listening. He had emptied a tin of baked beans into the bowl and was now sprinkling parmesan cheese on top.

"Been making this since I was a boy!" he exclaimed. "Know exactly what I'm doing!"

At that moment, Mrs Rocket walked past the kitchen window. Billy noticed that his dad wasn't really looking at what he was pouring into the bowl any more.

"But Dad..." said Billy a little louder, as Mr Bonkers tipped half a bag of salt and a jar of anchovies into the mix.

"Pish!" Mr Bonkers snorted, adding a jar of extra-hot lime pickle and a large pinch of dried red chillies. "I'm in total control of the situation!"

"That's what I'm worried about," groaned Billy.

"A spoonful of super-duper-horrifically-hot curry paste!" said Mr Bonkers, seizing the jar from the cupboard and taking off the lid.

At that moment, Mrs Rocket noticed Mr Bonkers standing in the window. She winked and mouthed "Happy birthday" at him.

Mr Bonkers went pink…and emptied the entire jar of curry paste into the bowl.

"Um, Dad, I don't think you meant to do that!" said Billy in alarm.

Mr Bonkers blinked a few times. Then he grabbed a wooden spoon and stirred the mixture until it was a gooey, reddish-brown paste.

"Nonsense," he said. "Piffle! Tried and tested for generations."

"But Dad—"

"My father before me, and his father before him," continued Mr Bonkers. "Sniff that, Billy. That'll put hairs on your chest!" He held the bowl out with an eager smile.

Billy took a cautious sniff and then backed away, coughing and sneezing violently. He felt pretty sure that it had just burned some of his nostril hairs away.

"But Dad," he spluttered, his eyes streaming. "That's… that's…"

"I know, I know," said Mr Bonkers. "Best thing you ever smelled, right?

The Fart Fumigation

No need to thank me, son. This'll teach Mr Rocket a thing or two about barbecues!"

He raced out into the garden, carrying the potent bowl of sauce. As soon as Billy had stopped coughing, he followed. Mr Bonkers had found another spatula and was now elbowing his way through the crowd around the barbecue.

"Make way, make way," he said. "King of the barbecue sausage coming through!"

Mr Rocket was busily turning sausages over the glowing coals. Mr Bonkers stood beside him and smeared the sticky, dark sauce all over the first sausage.

At that moment, there was a scream from the other side of the garden. Wasps from the nest next door were buzzing over the fence, drawn by the smell of food.

Mrs Rocket was flapping her hands in the air and squealing.

"Help!" she cried. "A wasp went down my dress!"

"I'll help!" cried all the dads at once, leaping towards Mrs Rocket.

The barbecue was completely abandoned. And that's when Billy had his brilliant idea.

His sister's pink pants were still in his pocket. But what if they were to accidentally fall onto the barbecue?

I'll just say I was leaning over to try the sauce, said Billy to himself.

I would like to point out that you should

The Fart Fumigation

absolutely never, under any circumstances, try to burn anything except food on a barbecue. But then you probably don't need to destroy your sister's pants.

Billy sneaked over to the barbecue and picked up a pair of tongs. Then he carefully took the pants out of his pocket and used the tongs to slip them onto the grill.

At first, nothing happened.

"Come on, *come on*," Billy urged the fire.

The mums were petting Cedric and the dads were still busy with the wasp, but Billy knew it was only a matter of time before they all came back. Then he noticed a tiny part of the white frill growing darker. Any minute now the pants would burst into flames. He would be saved! Just a few more seconds…

"Look out!" shouted Mr Rocket.

He leaped across to the barbecue and dived at the grill with his spatula. With a flick of his wrist, the pants were flipped off the grill and back into Billy's hands.

But Mr Rocket's spatula had also caught the edge of a sauce-smeared sausage. It somersaulted through the air, right into the welcoming jaws of Cedric, who gulped it down with one swallow.

Mr Rocket looked at Billy curiously. "Nice pants," he said with a chuckle.

"THEY'RE NOT...MY...PANTS!"

exclaimed Billy, going bright red.

They were a little bit scorched at the edge, but they were nowhere near damaged enough. Mrs Bonkers would still say he had to wear them.

Billy glared at Mr Rocket and stomped into the house. Betty, who had seen the whole thing, followed him.

"What's so bad about my pants, anyway?" she demanded as Billy walked into the kitchen.

"They're fine – for you!" said Billy, stuffing them back into his pocket. "What about when I have to get changed for sports at school?"

"No one will even be looking at your pants!" Betty scoffed.

"Right!" shouted Billy. "Because I won't be wearing them!"

Betty opened her mouth to reply, but then she glanced out of the kitchen window and forgot what she had been going to say.

The Fart Fumigation

Cedric was standing in the middle of the garden. A few moments ago, he had been wearing the satisfied look of a dog who has successfully stolen a sausage. But suddenly his expression had changed. At first he just looked curious. Then his hairy eyebrows raised in concern. Finally his face definitely registered alarm. Something was *very wrong*.

"Can you hear that?" said Betty.

Even through the closed window, the rumbling sound of Cedric's stomach was as loud as thunder. The sausage sauce was slipping into his belly, and something noxious and potent was brewing...

***

At this point, it is only fair to warn you that I'm afraid something extremely indelicate is about to happen. If you are a sensitive sort of person, stop reading now! Put down this book and go and do something else. Fly a kite. Build a mud pie. On no account should you read about the following unpleasantness unless you are feeling very, very brave.

***

As Billy watched, Cedric's whole body gave a little shudder. Then his back legs jumped apart, his bottom rose as if he was standing on tiptoes, and there was a gurgling, erupting sort of sound.

BLURRGURROWWSPLEECHARP!

Cedric let forth the most terrifically whiffy fart that Billy had ever known. It was an eruption of gigantic proportions. Billy saw it puff into the air like a small, green mushroom cloud.

It rose slightly and hovered above the people in the garden. Its surface looked as if it was boiling, just like a pan of water before you add the spuds.

Suddenly, everyone started gasping for air. Mr Bonkers dropped to his knees, clutching at his throat. Mr Rocket's eyes rolled in their sockets and he fell backwards into Mrs Bonkers's petunias.

All around the garden, people collapsed as soon as the stench of the toxic fart cloud reached them. A few seconds later,

only Cedric, Billy and Betty were still conscious. Cedric was standing stock still in the middle of the garden, his eyes like saucers.

Billy felt himself starting to panic.

The Fart Fumigation

"What are we going to do?" he cried. "If we go out there we'll be knocked out! That's poisonous gas!"

Betty thought hard. "We have to stop that cloud escaping," she said. "If it gets into the town, there'll be chaos."

"But how can we stop it?" Billy asked, gazing out at the fart cloud.

It was turning from green to a sort of bruised purple. It looked as if it might explode. Each plant it passed withered and shrivelled. It paused over Dad's new leaf blower, and the plastic on the handle started to bubble.

"Wait a minute!" said Betty. "I think I might have an idea!"

She raced upstairs and came back with Billy's goldfish, Snapper, in his round fish bowl.

"Voila!" she said. "What is this?"

"It's a fish bowl," said Billy. "But I'm not sending Snapper out there. The whiff might kill him! Besides, what could a goldfish possibly do to help?"

"It's a fish bowl..." Betty repeated patiently, "...or a fart-proof gas mask!"

"A what?" said Billy.

"All we have to do is empty the water – and Snapper – into another bowl," said Betty. "Then you can put the fish bowl on your head to protect you, and go out there and deal with the fart. Simple!"

The Fart Fumigation

"Hang on a minute!" said Billy. "How exactly am I supposed to deal with the fart?"

"You'll think of something," Betty replied.

Billy wasn't so sure, but someone had to stop that fart cloud, and no one else was volunteering.

"OK, I'll do it," he declared. "And if I don't make it, you can have your old pants back."

He tipped Snapper into the fruit bowl with some water, and then Betty turned the fish bowl over and plopped it over Billy's head.

"Can you breathe?" she asked.

Billy nodded, and the fish bowl wobbled around and steamed up. Soon all that Betty could see were Billy's eyes peering out at her.

"Quick!" she said, pushing Billy out through the back door and then slamming it shut.

Billy raced across the garden, jumping over the unconscious bodies of his parents and neighbours. Suddenly he spotted the new leaf blower, and a brilliant, mind-blowing, brain-dazzling idea popped into his head.

The Fart Fumigation

"Dad's new leaf blower has a suck function!" he yelled through the fish bowl at Betty. "Maybe it can suck the fart cloud up!"

"I can't hear a word you're saying," mouthed Betty from inside the house. "But I bet it's worth a try!"

Billy grabbed the leaf blower, hit the **ON** switch and then pressed the large red button. As the machine started to suck, Billy lifted it above his head and aimed it at the looming fart cloud. There was a slurping, gurgling **SHWURGHH**, and then the dark cloud of dog-bottom gas started to stretch out.

Billy Bonkers

It grew longer and thinner until it looked like a giant, stinky slug. Slowly but surely, the leaf blower began to draw it in.

When every last putrid particle was inside the leaf blower, Billy lowered the machine, his arms aching.

"Phew!" he said, pulling off the goldfish bowl and wiping his forehead.

Behind him, Betty opened the door a crack.

"Did it work?" she called.

Right at that moment, the leaf blower started to shudder. It was making a straining, stretching sound.

"The fart cloud's too much for it!" cried Billy.

"It's going to blow!"

There was no time to lose! He ran to the side of the garden as fast as he could, pointed the leaf blower over the fence and stuck the nozzle into the buzzing wasps' nest next door. Then he hit the red button and changed the function from "suck" to "blow".

VUHWHUM!

The poisonous fart cloud escaped – straight into the wasps' nest. The buzzing stopped immediately.

Then there was a series of tiny thunks as hundreds of wasps dropped out of their nest to the ground below.

Each and every one of them had been knocked unconscious by the reeking fart cloud, which was now safely contained in their nest.

"Hooray!" cheered Billy, punching the air. "It worked!"

Behind him, everyone was sitting up and shaking their heads. Betty removed the bowl full of sausage sauce before Mr Bonkers could try to use it again.

The Fart Fumigation

"Oh Billy!" said Mrs Rocket, stumbling woozily towards him. "You've saved us! My hero!"

She planted a large, wet kiss on Billy's cheek and Mr Bonkers sprang to his side.

"As a matter of fact, it was my leaf blower that carried out the job," he said. "And of course, Billy's my son. The Bonkers brain, that's what did the trick!"

Mrs Rocket gave him a dazzling smile.

"I think it's about time for something to eat, Sausage," said Mrs Bonkers in a loud voice. "And a round of applause for Billy!"

"I guess I just did what I had to," said Billy modestly.

Now, I expect that you are wondering what happened to Cedric, who caused the Great Fart in the first place. Well, throughout the fart fumigation, he had remained standing in the same position, staring straight ahead. Nothing of that size or malodorous stench had ever escaped from his bottom before, and he was in deep dog-shock. When the neighbours started to applaud Billy, Cedric blinked and looked around. He didn't remember coming into this garden. He didn't remember the humungous poisonous fart. He didn't even remember his own name.

The pong of the super-powered fart had completely wiped his memory!

While no one was looking, Cedric crept

out of the garden and down the street. He didn't know why, but something told him that he needed to get as far away from that garden as possible.

Billy was the hero of the hour, and that afternoon he ate enough charred sausages to sink a small battleship.

And maybe they gave him extra brain-power, because that afternoon he even thought of a plan to get rid of the pink pants once and for all.

But that's another story...

THE END

Billy Bonkers

and the
Town Treasure

Billy Bonkers was a very bouncy sort of boy. He usually jumped out of bed in the morning and bounded down the stairs with a large breakfast on his mind. But this time, when his radio alarm went off, there was no bouncing. This time, it was still the middle of the night.

Billy Bonkers

The pants situation was getting desperate. Twice that weekend Billy had tried to get rid of his sister's frilly knickers, and twice he had failed. Now he only had one clean pair of old pants left. Thanks to Mrs Bonkers's latest money-saving madness, unless he got rid of Betty's pants today, he'd be wearing the pink monstrosities to school on Monday morning.

So Billy had taken drastic steps. He had set his radio alarm clock for 2 a.m. The pants were under his pillow. All he had to do was flush them down the loo while no one was paying attention. Billy slithered out of bed, retrieved the pants and padded across the hall into the bathroom. He dropped the

pants into the toilet and used the loo brush to shove them as far down as he could. Then he pushed on the flush.

GALUMPHHSSSHHH!

Billy tiptoed back to his room, climbed into bed and lay down. A glorious feeling of wellbeing washed over him. The pants had gone forever! He smiled as he listened to the soothing tones of the night-time radio presenter Paddy Velvet.

"Yes, that's right listeners," Paddy was saying. *"Today's the day that the Town Park Campaign bites the dust. The pets have been evicted from Pets' Corner, the ducks have been thrown out of the duck pond and the diggers are moving in."*

In all the excitement of the weekend, Billy had forgotten about the plans for the town park. Mayor Glutbucket had agreed to sell it to a rich developer

so that it could be turned into a concrete car park. Mr and

Mrs Bonkers had joined the campaign against the plans, but no one had been able to raise enough money.

The Town Treasure

"First they'll be filling in the duck pond with concrete, and then they'll bulldoze the kids' playground," continued the voice of Paddy Velvet. "We spoke to Mayor Glutbucket last week and here's what he had to say."

The pompous voice of Mayor Glutbucket seeped out of the radio. "Of course it's most regrettable, but this town needs the money."

"But the campaigners have been trying to raise the funds to beat the developer's offer," said Paddy Velvet. "Couldn't you give them just a little more time?"

"Sadly it's out of the question," said Mayor Glutbucket, who didn't sound very sad at all. "Besides, this is progress. A large concrete car park is far more useful than a few swings. Harrumph!"

"You heard it here first, folks," said Paddy. "Say goodbye to the town park…"

Billy switched off the radio. He drifted

back to sleep and dreamed of
Mayor Glutbucket being chased
by an angry giant duck.

***

When Billy woke up
again, light was shining
through his curtains. He
yawned and looked at his alarm
clock. It was still only 5 a.m. What
had woken him up?

Then he heard voices in the street
outside. On Billy's street no one ever got
up this early on a Sunday.

"Something's going on," Billy said to
himself.

He opened the curtains and peered
down into the street. He could see three
large workmen in blue boiler suits. They

were standing around an open drain and
shaking
their
heads
at one
another.

Billy
pulled on his
slippers and
went out onto
the landing. He could hear Mr Bonkers's
rumbling snores and Mrs Bonkers's steady
breaths. Betty's door was firmly shut. Billy
tiptoed downstairs, opened the front door
and went out to the pavement.

Now that he was closer, he could see that
one of the workmen was plump, one of them
was chubby and one of them was definitely
– I'm afraid there's no other word for it –
rotund.

"Hello," said the plump workman as he joined them. "You're up early, young man."

"You too," said Billy. "Is there something wrong?"

"The council has had a report of a blockage in these ancient water pipes," said Chubby. "We've come down to investigate."

Billy peered into the open drain. It looked

The Town Treasure

dark and cold. A narrow ladder descended into blackness.

"Do you have to go down there?" he asked.

"We're supposed to," said the rotund workman. "The only trouble is…"

He patted his tummy and chuckled. "These drains were made hundreds of years ago," the plump workman explained. "We can't fit!"

Billy thought that this sounded very interesting.

And he had never seen the inside of a drain before.

"I'll go down for you, if you like," he said. "I'm small enough."

"That's very kind of you," said Chubby. "All you have to do is find out what the blockage is. Then we can report back to the depot."

"You should wear a boiler suit," said the rotund one.

He took his own suit off and Billy climbed into it. He had to roll up the legs and sleeves ten times each.

The plump workman handed Billy a yellow hard hat and a little torch.

The Town Treasure

"Good luck!"
he said.

Billy stepped onto
the narrow ladder
and started to climb
down into the tiny
drainpipe.

Above him, the
heads of the three workmen
blocked the light as they peered down.

"Now remember, don't touch anything,"
they called as Billy disappeared from
sight. "Just look for the blockage and then
come back."

"I will!" called
Billy.

"Will…will…will
…" called
the echo.

Billy reached the bottom of the ladder and started to crawl along the thin pipe on his hands and knees. The torch made a tiny circle of light in the ancient tunnel. There was a damp, musty smell in the air.

As he reached a bend in the pipe, Billy paused. One of the bricks in the wall was sticking out at an odd angle.

That's weird, thought Billy.

Up until that moment, Billy had no intention of touching anything in the grimy pipe. He just wanted to find the blockage and then go back. But something

about the brick made him feel curious. He
reached out and gave it a good, hard tug.

CRASH!

Something that had been hidden behind
the brick came tumbling down beside Billy.
Something large and black and heavy.

Billy picked up the mysterious object.
It was an old-fashioned
three-cornered
hat, and inside the
hat was a heavy
metal box. Billy
shook it and it
rattled.

"Bound to be
locked," he said
aloud.

"Locked…locked…locked…" said the echo.

But the lid opened easily and Billy gasped.

If you have ever met an archaeologist, you'll know that they are very interested in ancient objects that they dig up out of the ground. Well, if an archaeologist had been with Billy at that moment, I can guarantee that he or she would have fainted with excitement. Because what Billy saw inside the box was a pile of shiny gold coins!

"WOW!" said Billy.

"WOWOWOWOW . . ." said the echo.

They must have been down here for hundreds of years! As Billy gaped at them, he remembered something that he had learned at school.

The Town Treasure

"Mick Slurpin!" he shouted.

"Urpin…urpin…urpin…" wailed the echo.

The teachers at Billy and Betty's school hated telling the story of Mick Slurpin. It meant that they had to stop thinking about sums and spellings for a while. But the children loved hearing the old tale.

Mick Slurpin was a wicked highwayman who had lived in the town hundreds of years ago. He'd held up countless carriages and stolen bagfuls of jewels, silver and gold. Legend said that he had buried his treasure in a secret hiding place somewhere in the town.

"I've found the treasure!" Billy said to himself, his eyes nearly popping out of his head as he imagined all the snacks he'd be able to buy with the coins.

A football pitch filled with pork pies, he thought. *A swimming pool full of*  *ice cream! A million bowls of porridge!* Billy's tummy rumbled expectantly.

Billy put the hat and the box under his yellow hard hat for safekeeping and then carried on crawling down the tunnel. At last he reached a T-junction, which was directly underneath another drain cover. And right in the place where the two sticks of the T met, something was stretched across the drain, stopping the water from flowing. Something pink...and frilly...and covered in kittens.

"Pants!" Billy exclaimed in horror.

"Your pants... pants...pants..." said the echo mockingly.

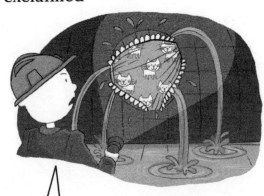

"THEY'RE NOT...MY...PANTS!"

said Billy.

The workmen had told him not to touch anything, but Billy knew he couldn't leave the pants there for someone else to find. The whole street would discover that Billy's pink pants had blocked the drains! He grabbed the elasticated waistband and tugged as hard as he could.

The pants wouldn't budge.

"Nooo!" groaned Billy.

He pulled. He heaved.
He strained and
wheezed and groaned.
And then, just when he
was giving up hope . . .

TWANG!

The pants came loose and the water was
released.

WHOOSH!

Billy went
shooting
upwards on
top of the jet of
pent-up water.

"**HEELLLPPP!**" cried Billy as he hurtled into the air.

His hard hat smashed into the drain cover, which flew off. Billy was carried aloft on a high plume of water, rising above the street.

He clutched his hard hat tightly and looked down. He could just make out the surprised upturned faces of the workmen.

"**Oooh!**" said the plump one as Billy flew over his head. "**Ahhh!**" cried the rotund one, as the G-force ripped Billy's boiler suit off and tore the pants from his hand. "**Ohhh!**" said Chubby as Billy became a speck in the distance.

He was catapulted over roofs, chimneys and gardens. For a moment he thought that things couldn't get any worse…and then he started to fall. Seconds later, Billy was hurtling towards a posh house in the most expensive part of town.

When you drop a piece of toast on your mum's new carpet, it will always land butter-side down. When your alarm clock doesn't go off in the morning, it'll be the only day that your school bus is on time. And if you are Billy Bonkers, and flying headlong towards a large roof, you will absolutely always plop headfirst down the chimney.

Billy plummeted down the sooty brick tunnel at top speed. His first thought was: *I hope there's no f-i-r-e!*

Then: *Hur-ray! I'm slo-wing do-wn.*

Then: *OUCH!*

The chimney was narrowest at its bottom, and Billy was widest in his middle. When the widest part of Billy arrived at the narrowest part of the chimney, only one thing could happen. Yes, you guessed it. Billy got stuck.

Luckily the fire wasn't lit, because his head was dangling into the grate. Billy blinked the soot out of his eyes and peered into the room. It was a bedroom, and worse still, someone was asleep in the bed. The blanket was stretched over an enormous belly. The man in the bed was wearing red stripy pyjamas and a lot of heavy gold chains around his neck.

The Town Treasure

"Mayor Glutbucket!" Billy gasped.

The mayor was fast asleep and making bubbling snoring noises.

I've got to get out of here! thought Billy. He wiggled and jiggled, but apart from dislodging a bit more soot, nothing happened.

Then the mayor made a harrumphing, galumphing sound. It was the sort of sound that a hippo might make when it was settling down for the night. Billy froze.

"Just one more pork pie, Mrs Glutbucket …" murmured the mayor, smacking his lips.

Billy looked around in alarm, but there was no one else in the room. Then the truth dawned on him. Mayor Glutbucket was talking in his sleep.

At first, Billy didn't listen. All he wanted to do was to get out of there as fast as possible. He squirmed and writhed, and lots more soot fell down around him. But he still couldn't get his arms free. Then he heard something that made his ears prick up. (Or down, in Billy's case, as he was still the wrong way up.) In between snores, Mayor Glutbucket was saying something very interesting indeed.

"Silly old town park…*huruffuffle*… lovely concrete car park…*murffle*… mustn't let the fundraisers win…tell the developer…*hnnrumfle*…split the profits fifty-fifty…*phushh*…sell the swimming pool…*mmmggguhhh*…concrete the lot… *harrumph*…retire to Barbados…"

Billy's mouth fell open, which is an odd feeling when you're upside down. Mayor Glutbucket was behind the evil development! He was planning to sell off the town piece by piece to line his own pockets.

"They'll never raise the money to stop me in time…" said the mayor, giving a loud chuckle.

We'll see about that! thought Billy.

He gave another tremendous wriggle. This time, perhaps because he was fired up by anger, he managed to free his arm. He landed in the grate with a loud bump, and the hard hat fell off. The three-cornered hat

dropped out and the box burst open, scattering gold coins into the grate.

Billy squatted down, gathering up the coins and shoving them into his pyjama pockets.

"Wh-what?" exclaimed the mayor, sitting up in bed. "Who's there?" His voice sounded weak and trembly.

Billy bit his lip and stared at the three-cornered hat and the gold coins. How on earth was he going to explain this?

Now, if you've ever been put on the spot, you'll know how hard it is to think of the right thing to say in that split second. Often you don't think of the right thing until several days later, when the moment has passed and everyone has got bored and gone home. But very, very occasionally, you think of a brilliant phrase at the perfect moment. And at that precise second, Billy suddenly knew exactly what to say. He grabbed the black hat and shoved it on his head. Then he pressed the torch against the underside of his chin and switched it on.

"I am the ghost of Mick Slurpin!" he croaked.

The mayor screamed. All he could see was the weirdly lit floating head of a long-dead highwayman. He screamed again.

"No one can hear you," rasped Billy, hoping he was right. "I am here to haunt you, Mayor Glutbucket!"

He took a step out of the grate towards the bed. The mayor gathered his blanket under his chin and whimpered, "Wh-why m-me?"

Billy took another step forward. "You have cheated our town," he groaned. "You are going to destroy the park!"

"I'm s-sorry!" the mayor blubbed. "I'll put it right, I promise! I'll stop the development."

Billy let out a long, sinister hiss. "You'll let the fundraisers buy the park?" he asked.

"Yes, yes, I promise! Just leave me alone!"

"Very well," Billy growled. "I'll let you off this once. But if you ever try to cheat the town again, I'll be back to haunt you forever!"

The Town Treasure

"I won't! I won't!" wibbled Mayor Glutbucket.

"Now lie down and close your eyes," said Billy.

The Mayor collapsed backwards and lay still, his eyes squeezed shut. Billy picked up the empty box and the yellow hard hat, and then scooted out through the bedroom door. He raced down the stairs, out into the street and back home as fast as he could.

When Billy got there, the workmen had replaced the drain covers and gone back to the council depot. Billy pulled the coins out of his pocket and put them back

117

into the box. He placed the box beside the milk on his front doorstep. Then he picked up the pen and paper that Mrs Bonkers used to write complaints to the milkman. He wrote a note and put it on top of the box.

Then he let himself into the house, ran upstairs and darted into his bedroom – seconds before his mother's door opened! He let out a sigh of relief.

"Where on earth has all this soot come from?" he heard her say. "Lordy lorks, it's all over the stairs!"

"Chimney must need a sweep," said Mr Bonkers's voice.

"Don't be silly, Sausage. We don't have a chimney."

Billy heard her opening the front door.

"I'll just get the milk and – oh!"

SMASH! went the milk bottle.

"**EEEK!**" went Mrs Bonkers.

And in his room, Billy chuckled again.

By the time he had brushed the soot off his pyjamas and bounced downstairs, the box of gold coins was in the middle of

the breakfast table and the family was in uproar. Mr Bonkers was striding around the table, shaking his head and shouting at the top of his voice. Betty was gabbling at a

hundred miles an hour, trying to work out where the money could have come from. And Mrs Bonkers was on the phone to the mayor.

"...gold coins on the doorstep! Secret friends! The world's gone mad!"

"...and even Roger Rocket doesn't have that much money and besides which it has to be someone who would have gold coins and..."

"...and yes, Mayor Glutbucket, there is definitely enough for us to buy the park for the community... What's that?... We can?... You will? Oh lordy lorks, that's wonderful!"

Billy smiled and poured himself an extra-large bowl of porridge.

Mrs Bonkers put down the phone and clasped her hands together. Tears of joy poured down her face

"It's amazing!" she cried. "The Mayor says that he will let us buy the park instead of the developer – and he is going to pay for a brand-new play park out of his own pocket! Oh, Sausage!"

She threw her arms around Mr Bonkers and planted a smacker of a kiss right on his lips. Betty groaned and Billy put his hands over his eyes. "Oh pur-lease," said Betty. "Tell me when they've stopped," said Billy. Just then,

he heard a faint tinkle. A single gold coin had fallen from his pocket. His parents weren't looking, so he bent down to pick it up. But as he added it to the pile in the middle

of the table, he saw his sister's eagle eyes watching him. She raised her eyebrows questioningly. Billy put his finger over his lips.

"Tell you later," he whispered.

"The only thing you'll be doing later is getting dressed, young man," said Mrs Bonkers. "I want you to go and put on your best clothes and get ready to meet the mayor. Oh, and Billy, I found your pants lying on the street outside, all wet and muddy. I'll put them in the wash for you to wear to school tomorrow. I can't imagine how they got there!"

People in Billy's street talked about what happened next for years. One minute they were having a lovely Sunday morning lie-in. Next moment, windows rattled, doors shook in their frames, pictures fell off walls and animals dived for cover. The bellow was so loud that it was even reported on alien news as a gigantic earthquake on some unidentified planet:

THE END

Billy Bonkers

'Utterly bonkers!
A riot of fun! I loved it!'
– Harry Enfield

Mad stuff happens with
Billy Bonkers! Whether
he's flying through the
air propelled by porridge
power, or blasting
headfirst into a chocolate-
covered planet – life is
never boring with Billy,
it's BONKERS!

Three hilarious stories
in one from an award-
winning author and
illustrator team.

978 1 84616 151 3 £4.99 pbk

978 1 40830 357 3 £5.99 pbk

ORCHARD BOOKS
www.orchardbooks.co.uk

Max and Molly's Guide To Trouble!

Meet Max and Molly: terrorising the neighbourhood really extremely politely...

Max and Molly's guides guarantee brilliantly funny mayhem and mischief as we learn how to be a genius, catch a criminal, build an abominable snowman and stop a Viking invasion!

978 I 40830 519 5 £4.99 Pbk
978 I 40831 572 9 eBook

978 I 40830 520 I £4.99 Pbk
978 I 40831 573 6 eBook

978 I 40830 521 8 £4.99 Pbk
978 I 408 31574 3 eBook

978 I 40830 522 5 £4.99 Pbk
978 I 408 31575 0 eBook

ORCHARD BOOKS

www.orchardbooks.co.uk